christmas, 1993
For my talented
daughter,
Maria

P9-DOA-010

FIFTH WORLD TALES
Stories for all children from the many peoples of America.

The River that Gave Gifts

an Afro American story
Written and Illustrated by Margo Humphrey

For Brian, Alkebu-lan and
Oronde whose spirits gave
me the inspiration for
this book

CHILDREN'S BOOK PRESS / IMPRENTA DE LIBROS INFANTILES
SAN FRANCISCO, CALIFORNIA

Revised edition © 1987, original edition © 1978 by Children's Book Press
All rights reserved. Printed in Hong Kong through Interprint, San Francisco
CIP data mav be found on page 24.

IN A HOUSE
on the side of a country meadow,
there lived a girl named Yanava.
She was a beautiful dark brown child
who found it difficult to make things
with her hands.

But she thought about many things, and what
her hands could not create, her mind could.

3

Her nearby friends were Oronde, Kengee and Jey. They had
played together all their lives, and they had one special thing
in common: they all loved Neema, the wise old woman of
the town, who had always listened to them and answered
their questions.

The children knew that Neema loved colors because of the
fine quilts that she made. They also knew that her eyes
were growing dim. So they decided they would each give
her something that showed their love before the time came
when she would not be able to see.

Jey looked through the colorful buttons in her old button jar and found some that her grandmother had given her. They were worn with age and all golden on the edges like the setting sun. Jey chose the loveliest buttons of all and strung them on a chain for Neema.

Kengee made ribbon bows from the bits and pieces of bright cloth that she found in her mother's sewing box. She cut and put them together just so, for Kengee cared very much for Neema.

Oronde built a box to hold all of Neema's precious
things. He carefully chose each piece of wood.
He fitted the pieces together and made a handle so
that the box would be easy for Neema to carry.
Then he polished the box until it shone with all
the love he had put into making it.

While Jey, Kengee and Oronde were working on their gifts, Yanava went to her favorite place to think about what she could give Neema.

She sat down beside the river which flowed through her yard. "What should the present be?" she asked herself. "Should it be large or small?" And most importantly, "What does Neema need the most?"

It was quiet and peaceful. The river sparkled ever so brightly from the sun. It was as if someone had thrown diamonds upon the water as it flowed by.

Soon the river began to whisper,
"Take me into your hands.
Take me into your hands."
The murmur of the river began
to send her into a peaceful sleep.

The river was old and wise with the wisdom of the ancient ones. The river knew the gift that Yanava should give to Neema, the elder.

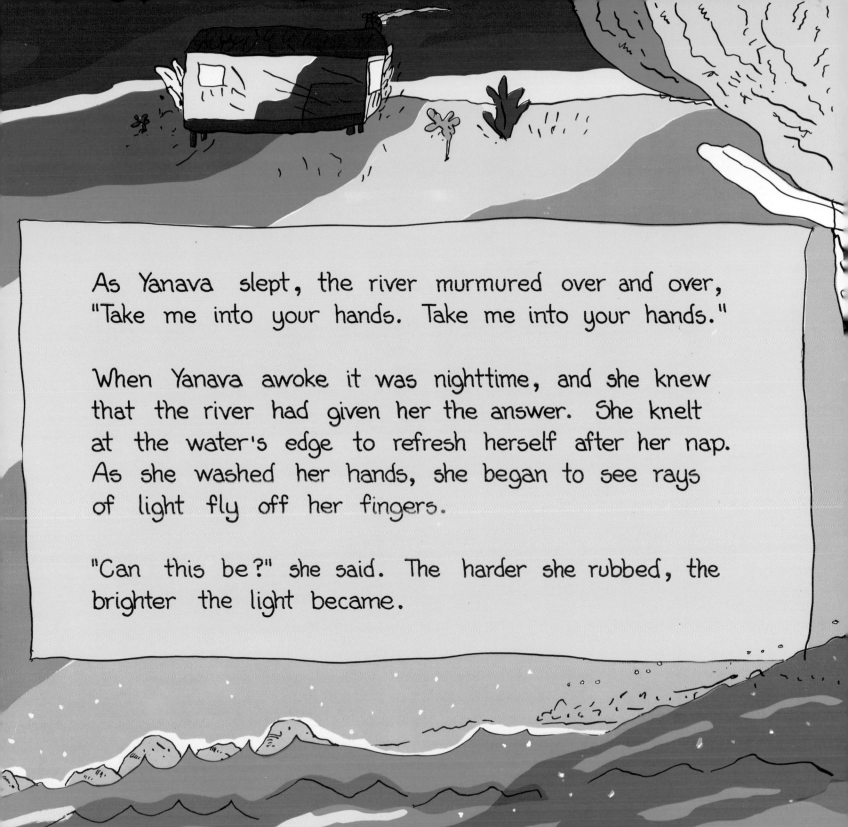

As Yanava slept, the river murmured over and over, "Take me into your hands. Take me into your hands."

When Yanava awoke it was nighttime, and she knew that the river had given her the answer. She knelt at the water's edge to refresh herself after her nap. As she washed her hands, she began to see rays of light fly off her fingers.

"Can this be?" she said. The harder she rubbed, the brighter the light became.

The river whispered, "You, Yanava, beautiful black child, have the gift of light. Let me show you. Hold out your hands."

She held out her hands, and the light streaming from her fingers changed into different colors.

From her thumbs came the color red, the color of happiness. From her first fingers came the color yellow, the color of the sun which is the soul of all living things. From her second fingers came the color green, the color of life. From her third fingers came the color blue, the color of birth and water. And from her little fingers came the color violet, the color of royalty.

The day finally arrived for the presentation of Neema's gifts.

First to enter the dimly lighted room was Oronde, who presented the box he had made. It was a beautiful box, but Neema could barely see it. "Thank you," she said.

Next came Kengee with her ribbon bows woven together into a colorful piece to hang on the wall. Then came Jey with her old buttons strung on an elegant chain. But it was difficult for Neema to see these gifts in the dim light of the room.

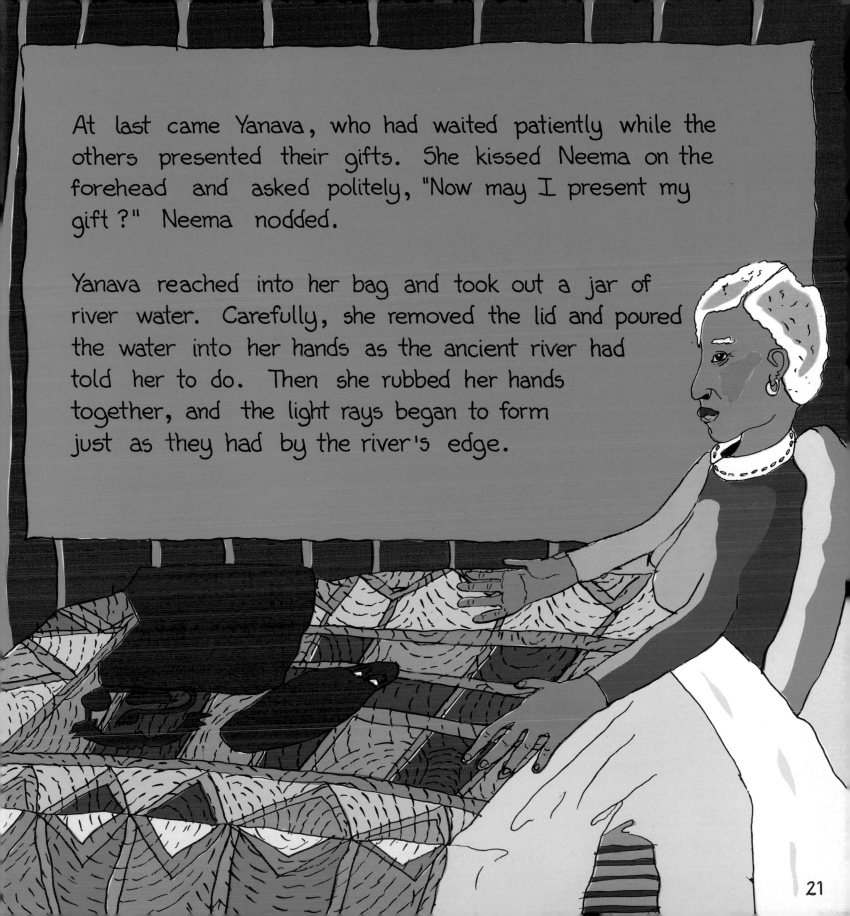

At last came Yanava, who had waited patiently while the others presented their gifts. She kissed Neema on the forehead and asked politely, "Now may I present my gift?" Neema nodded.

Yanava reached into her bag and took out a jar of river water. Carefully, she removed the lid and poured the water into her hands as the ancient river had told her to do. Then she rubbed her hands together, and the light rays began to form just as they had by the river's edge.

21

Yanava stood with her hands extended as the colors of the rainbow flowed from her fingers. The dark room was transformed into a vision of color, and Neema could see. *Neema could see!*

Now Neema could see all of her presents because of Yanava's special gift ~ the gift of light.

About the Story and Its Creator

The River that Gave Gifts is a revealing story about the meaning of respect in the Afro American community. Neema in her old age is honored, rather than forgotten or rejected. Her wisdom is seen to be akin to the wisdom of the river itself, which dates back to the time of the remotest ancestors. The children show their respect for Neema by presenting her with gifts. The gifts are more than just physical objects, for they incorporate all the love which the children feel for the old woman.

The story is also a lesson about the validity of different kinds of achievement. Orande, Kengee and Jey are skillful with their hands. Yanava is not. She works instead with her mind and spirit, and her gift makes it possible for Neema to genuinely receive the gifts of all the others.

Margo Humphrey was born in Oakland, California. Her mother, who had studied to become a hat designer, was very proud of her young daughter's artistic talent and always made sure that she had water colors and drawing tablets. After special high school courses at the College of Arts and Crafts in Oakland, Ms. Humphrey went on to attend Merritt College and Stanford University where she obtained her master's degree in fine arts. "The way was never easy for her," her mother said. "Sometimes she had to drop out of school for months in order to earn the money to pay for her studies. But she was determined to continue."

Ms. Humphrey has been very much influenced by the art and culture of Africa. (The names in the story are African, as is much of the feeling and color.) After completing this book, Ms. Humphrey spent several weeks in Senegal, studying the architecture, fabric printing and carving of different tribal peoples. She currently teaches at the University of California (Santa Cruz).

Series Editor	Harriet Rohmer
Hand Lettering	Roger I Reyes
Book Design	Harriet Rohmer, Robin Cherin, Roger I Reyes
Production	Robin Cherin

Library of Congress Cataloging-in-Publication Data
Humphrey, Margo. The river that gave gifts.
   (Fifth world tales)
   Summary: Four children each make their own special gift to the beloved elder woman of the town.
   [1. Afro-Americans—Fiction.   2. Gifts—Fiction.   3. Friendship—Fiction]   I. Title.   II. Series.
PZ7.H897Ri 1986   [Fic]   86-17097
ISBN 0-89239-027-1

24